WRESTLING TROLLS

FUN&GAMES

Grab paper, pens, scissors, a friend
and complete the wrestling challenges!

DRAW A TROLL
STEP BY STEP

1. Trolls look like they're made of rock, so start with penciling an odd stone shape.

2a.

Add the head, nose and limbs in equally rock-like shapes. Don't forget the tail!

2b.

3. Now grab a marker and trace your sketch.

4.

Finally add colours and bumps, warts, mushrooms, twigs, hairs and what have you. Is your troll wearing pelts or a costume? A hat or dreadlocks? Jewellery or moss? (Probably all of the above.)

DRAW A COMPLETELY UNEXPECTED WRESTLER!

With your eyes closed, draw a random shape on a piece of paper. Open your eyes and use pencils and colours to turn your squiggle into a wrestler. Does it look like a troll or an orc? A goblin or a giant?

Play with a friend. You can draw a funny shape for the other person to transform.

I'VE DONE THIS!

A REAL BIG ROCK

GRAB SOME ROCKS AND MAKE A MODEL BIG ROCK FIGURE!

YOU WILL NEED:

1. A small, round rock for the head
2. A very small, oval rock for the nose (the knobblier the better)
3. A medium oval rock for the body
4. Thick twigs for the arms and legs
5. Scraps of fabric for his costume
6. A small piece of string with a frayed end for his tail
7. Tack or glue to stick them all together

I'VE DONE THIS!

by Elliot O'Connor

ROUND 4 — THE WRESTLING RING

DESIGN YOUR DREAM STADIUM FOR THE BATTLE OF THE GIANTS

DRAW AND LABEL:

- The ring
- Seats for lots of excited spectators
- Souvenir stands
- Food stalls
- Toilets
- Dressing rooms

Example by Twinkle on www.thestoryadventure.com

☐ I'VE DONE THIS!

GOBLIN MINE

ROUND 5

DANGER! MINE

Make a secret map of the goblins' mine to help Jack, Big Rock and Robin find their way to rescue Milo. Don't forget danger signs for lookout goblins and booby traps set by Govo — and any other obstacles you can think of.

☐ I'VE DONE THIS!

WRITE A LIMERICK

WRITE A LIMERICK IN SUPPORT OF YOUR FAVOURITE CHARACTER

Here's how you do it:

Lines 1, 2 and 5 rhyme with each other.

Lines 3 and 4 rhyme with each other.

The lines also have a special rhythm:

Lines 1, 2 and 5 all have this rhythm pattern:

da DUM da da DUM da da DUM.

Lines 3 and 4 are shorter. They go: da DUM da da DUM.

There once was a princess called Ava
A wrestler you couldn't find braver
In a vicious orc fight
She turned off the light
And not once did her courage waver

by Isapop on www.thestoryadventure.com

TROLL NAME GENERATOR

Use this chart, the first letter of your name and your birthday month to find your very own troll name.

A	HAIRY
B	SLIMY
C	WICKED
D	MIGHTY
E	NOISY
F	FEARSOME
G	TERRIBLE
H	HULKING
I	INVINCIBLE
J	FORMIDABLE
K	RUMBLING
L	MAMMOTH
M	FIERCE
N	POWERFUL
O	SUPER
P	MAGNIFICENT
Q	STUPENDOUS
R	AWESOME
S	STRONG
T	TOWERING
U	GOLDEN
V	TUMBLING
W	UGLY
X	HAIRY
Y	ROCKY
Z	SLIPPERY

JANUARY	EARTHQUAKE
FEBRUARY	CRASHER
MARCH	LANDSLIDE
APRIL	SMASHER
MAY	MOUNTAIN
JUNE	GRIP
JULY	HAYSTACK
AUGUST	ROAR
SEPTEMBER	TROLLIO
OCTOBER	HAMMER
NOVEMBER	THUMPER
DECEMBER	GIANT

MY TROLL NAME:

_____

_____

☐ I'VE DONE THIS!

To play, all you need is the start of a story, some friends to play with and your brain.

FORTUNATELY / UNFORTUNATELY STORY GAME

The first person starts the story, aloud to the whole group:

> "Once upon a time, Big Rock, the Wrestling Troll, was hungry for some rocks."

The next person continues the story with something UNFORTUNATE, relating to what they just heard:

> "UNFORTUNATELY, the evil Lord Veto had stolen all the rocks in the whole forest."

The next person changes the story with FORTUNATELY:

> "FORTUNATELY, Big Rock met up with Jack and Milo, and they found a big pile of rocks outside of the forest, next to a big blue lake."

And the story continues to alternate fortunately, unfortunately as each person adds to the story:

> "UNFORTUNATELY a big sea monster came out of the lake and starting chasing the three friends."

> "FORTUNATELY, Big Rock teamed up with Princess Ava (aka the Masked Avenger) and they were able to wrestle the monster back into the lake."

And on and on until it seems like a good time to end the story — either with a fortunate ending or an unfortunate one!

SO, HOW DOES YOUR STORY START?

☐ I'VE DONE THIS!

WRESTLING RING

Had fun with these games and want more Wrestling Trolls action?

There's more fun and games waiting for you right now on www.wrestlingtrolls.com, with free finger puppets to collect of your favourite characters!

Join the Wrestling Ring and get a free puppet of Big Rock to battle with. Plus, upload your creations from this section and you can also earn yourself other exclusive downloads.

Log on now to www.wrestlingtrolls.com

HUNK

CHAPTER 1

The old, battered-looking caravan, with WWT in big but faded letters on its side, rattled through the valley along the country road alongside a river.

'What's this place we're going to?' asked Robin, the ancient horse who pulled the caravan along.

'It's a town called Riverdam,' answered Milo, Manager of Waldo's Wrestling Trolls, as he held the reins. 'It's just along here, by the river. Around the next bend.'

The last remaining Wrestling Troll in Milo's team, Big Rock, ran around the caravan as it trundled along, throwing punches at the air and giving practice side kicks as he ran.

'Let me guess, there's a dam in the river next to it,' said Robin.

'Yes,' said Milo. 'How did you know?'

'The clue is in the name,' said Robin sarcastically.

'The Riverdam Slam!' said Jack, the nine-year-old boy and the team's Assistant Trainer, sitting next to Milo. 'It's only a small wrestling tournament but they say the crowds come from miles around. They're really keen on wrestling here.'

Just around the bend in the road, there was a nice little town – a few houses, with a large

wooden building in the middle.

'That's the place,' said Milo. 'That wooden building is the Town Hall where the event is to be held.'

As they drew nearer, they could see the dam, made of wood, right across the river. It looked like a bigger version of the sort of dam made by beavers: trees and logs intertwined with one another to keep back the water behind it.

Other caravans and some wagons had been parked on the green open space in front of the Town Hall. And, among them, was a carriage with the royal crest of the Kingdom of Weevil painted on the door.

'Princess Ava is here!' said Jack.

'And Sam Dent!' said Big Rock, equally pleased.

Princess Ava and the muscular figure of Sam Dent waved from the steps of the Town Hall.

Milo pulled the caravan to a halt and he and Jack jumped down. Princess Ava hugged them warmly, while Big Rock and Sam Dent bumped chests with big grins on their faces.

Although Ava was a princess and had to be always on her best and proper behaviour, now and then she managed to sneak away and wrestle as the Masked Avenger. Jack guessed that was her reason for being here at the Riverdam Slam, which she confirmed straight away. 'I'm here to take on Grit. She's a fantastic Wrestling Troll!

'Yes,' nodded Big Rock. 'Grit, great wrestler. Nice person too. She won't be easy.'

'I don't want things easy,' said Ava. 'I want a challenge!'

'You're taking a chance,' cautioned Jack. 'You could be unmasked.'

No one could ever know that Princess Ava was a wrestler, so she wore a full-face mask ... and the mask could only be taken off if she lost.

Princess Ava shook her head. 'I've seen Grit in the ring. She's good, but I can beat her.'

'Are you wrestling, Sam?' Jack asked.

'I was supposed to take on a Wrestling Orc called Slash,' sighed Sam, disappointed, 'but he says he wants to do tag wrestling with his orc partner, Burn.'

'Me supposed to fight Burn!' said Big Rock. 'Remember, Milo?'

'Yes, that's what the contract said,' nodded Milo. 'But you can't trust orcs. They don't keep their word.' Then his face lit up. 'Why don't you two take on Slash and Burn in a tag contest? It'll solve everything.'

'Brilliant!' said Sam. He turned to Big Rock.

'What do you say, Big Rock? You and me as tag partners?'

'Yes!' beamed Big Rock. 'We beat sneaky orcs.' And he made a fart noise to show how he felt about orcs.

'Who else is here?' asked Milo.

Princess Ava gave a sniff. 'There's a new wrestler called Hunk.'

'I don't know him,' frowned Milo. 'Where's he from?'

'Who knows?' shrugged Ava. 'He says he's a Wrestling Troll.' She gave a snort of derision. 'He's such a poser. He thinks he's so handsome!'

'He is,' said Sam.

'Well, yes, he is,' admitted Princess Ava. 'And he knows it.'

Robin joined them, intrigued by all this gossip. 'A handsome troll?' asked Robin, surprised.

'In fact he's a half-troll,' said Sam.

'Like Jack?' asked Milo.

'Not really,' said Sam. 'Hunk doesn't change into someone different like Jack does when he becomes Thud. Hunk is human from his head down to his knees. Then he's troll from the knees down.'

'He's got these great big hairy feet of which he's very proud,' said Princess Ava. 'He says they are an important part of his troll ancestry.' She gave a snort. 'You wait till you see him. Like I said, he's a poser. I don't think he's a real wrestler at all.'

'He must be if he's here for the tournament,' said Jack.

'That doesn't mean anything,' said Ava. 'Anyone can turn up and say they're a wrestler.'

'I think you're being unfair to him,' said Sam. 'He *looks* like a wrestler.' He half-turned and pointed. 'In fact, there he is now. That's Hunk.'

The others turned, and saw a very tall, powerful, muscular figure, dressed in a skintight pale blue leotard. He had blonde hair, and he was indeed very handsome – more like a film star than a wrestler. The other noticeable thing about him was his lower legs: from his knees to his toes he had thick, rock-like legs with enormous rocky feet and thick hairs sprouting out from them.

Hunk spotted the group and waved, heading towards them with a big welcoming grin on his face.

'Hi!' he called. 'My name's Hunk!' Then his face changed to an expression of awe. 'Wow!' he said. 'It's Big Rock! Please allow me to shake your hand!'

With that, Hunk moved towards Big Rock, his hand out. With a slightly bewildered expression on his face, Big Rock took Hunk's hand and Hunk shook it.

'I am such a fan of yours!' continued Hunk. 'I'm so glad I'll be able to watch you! Who are you up against?'

'Me and Sam Dent against orcs,' said Big Rock.

'Slash and Burn,' added Milo. 'Tag wrestling.'

'Wow!' said Hunk. 'That should be awesome!'

'Who are you wrestling?' asked Jack.

'Me?' said Hunk. 'I'm in the ring against Ug the Giant. We're first on the bill tomorrow.' He grinned. 'It should be fun! I love wrestling!

CHAPTER 2

The next morning, after breakfast, the gang went to the Town Hall. The crowds were already assembling in a queue by the box office to get their tickets, and Jack heard lots of excited whispers of 'There's Big Rock!' as they headed towards the wrestlers' entrance at the back. Big Rock stopped and waved at the crowd and shook hands (being careful not to squeeze too hard and hurt them). He pressed his thumbprint onto the pages of autograph books that the children in the crowd offered him.

'Nice place, nice people,' he commented as they walked through the back door and along the corridor towards the dressing rooms. Jack walked beside him, carrying a bag with Big

Rock's costume in.

Big Rock's costume was something that Jack guarded very carefully. It was very old, with lots of patches sewn onto it covering up holes in the cloth. In fact, sometimes Jack thought the costume was more patches than original material.

Sam Dent and Princess Ava were already there, as was a small girl troll.

'That's Grit,' Milo whispered to Jack.

'Hi, guys!' Sam Dent greeted them. He was already dressed in his black-and-white striped leotard, with a picture of a tiger on his chest. 'All ready, Big Rock?'

'Ready!' nodded Big Rock. 'Just putting my costume on.'

And he took the bag with his costume from Jack and disappeared behind a curtain.

'Where are the orcs?' asked Milo. 'I haven't seen them yet.'

'They say they're not mixing with us before the bout,' said Sam. 'They want to make their "big entrance".'

'Typical orcs!' snorted Milo. 'Always trying something to get an edge.'

He checked the order of bouts that was pinned up on the wall:

Hunk versus Ug the Giant
Grit versus the Masked Avenger
Tag event: Big Rock and Sam Dent versus
Slash and Burn

'Big Rock and Sam aren't on till last,' said Milo. 'We can watch the first two bouts from the hall. That'll give us a chance to see how good this Hunk character is.'

'And a chance to cheer on Princess ... er ... the Masked Avenger,' said Jack.

They told Big Rock and Sam they'd see them later, and then walked into the hall. It was nearly full already, but Robin had managed to grab a space at the back and they squeezed in beside him.

The three watched as the crowd continued filing into the hall and the rows of seats filled up. Some spectators had dressed up as their favourite wrestlers. There were at least ten people wearing costumes made to look like Big Rock's multi-patched one, with a picture of a mountain top on the front. Six or so had come dressed as Sam Dent; four girls had dressed up as Grit, two people perched one on top of the other inside a large sack that had 'Ug the Giant' written on it, and there were at least eight people dressed as orcs, complete with fake talons and with red eyeshadow painted around their eyes.

One person was wearing a mask in honour of the Masked Avenger. No one was dressed as Hunk, but Jack guessed that was because the half-troll was a new face on the scene, and no one knew enough about him yet.

By now the hall was absolutely packed. The house lights began to dim, and the harsh bright lights above the ring came on. Into the ring stepped the Master of Ceremonies, wearing a brightly coloured waistcoat and a big yellow bow tie.

'My lords, ladies and gentlemen!' he boomed,

his voice filling the hall. 'Welcome to the fantastic Riverdam Slam, featuring some of the greatest wrestlers on the scene today, as well as introducing some of the newest and up and coming wrestling stars of the future!'

At this the crowd erupted into cheers and stamped their feet and whistled. The Master of Ceremonies waved his hands asking for them to please be quiet. As an expectant hush settled over the crowd, the Master of Ceremonies once again beamed at them and made his announcement, but this time his voice had an apologetic tone.

'Today's programme was due to begin with a fantastic contest between Hunk, the half-troll, and Ug the Giant,' he announced. 'But, unfortunately, Ug was taken ill with stomach ache not long ago, and he's had to withdraw.'

At this, there were shouts and cries of disappointment from the crowd, but before it could get out of hand the Master of Ceremonies flashed a big smile and boomed into the microphone, drowning any unhappy noises.

'So instead we move to the next bout on the bill: a fantastically exciting match between that brilliant young rising star of Troll Wrestling – the truly formidable, and so far unbeaten . . . my lords, ladies and gentlemen, I give you . . . Grit!'

With that, the curtain at the back of the hall opened and the small, stocky figure of Grit appeared. She was about the same height as Princess Ava, but much wider, and much more muscular. Grit's wrestling costume of bright multi-coloured spangles twinkled and shone, the reflected light from the spangles merging

with the crystalline sheen of Grit's rocky and stony skin.

Grit waved at the crowd, who cheered the small troll loudly as she stomped down the aisle to the ring, and pulled herself into it through the ropes.

'Stomach ache?' queried Milo, puzzled over the news about Ug. 'That's unusual. Most of the giants I've met could eat anything without suffering stomach ache.'

'Something suspicious is going on there,' muttered Robin. 'I heard that Ug was seen having breakfast with Hunk.' He looked thoughtful. 'Remember what Princess Ava said about him? Could it just be coincidence that Ug then suffered stomach ache?' he asked. 'What better way for Hunk to avoid actually having to appear in the ring and prove whether he's a real wrestler or not, than by sneaking some stuff into Ug's breakfast.'

Jack looked around and saw Hunk standing at the back of another section of the hall, his attention fully on the ring in the middle. If he was disappointed at not being able to take part in the event, he didn't look it.

While Grit stood in one corner of the ring and waited, the MC took centre stage again.

'And now, Grit's opponent, that mystery wrestler who is only known as the Masked Avenger! Yes, my lords, ladies and gentlemen, she wears a mask to hide her identity. Who is she? Is she a famous star? Is she royalty? Is she a famous wrestler appearing under an assumed name? There will only ever be one way for her mask to come off and her identity to be known, and that is if she loses! If that happens, then the person who defeats her has the right to take the mask from her head! Will that be her fate today against Grit?'

At this, there rose a huge cheer from the crowd, along with shouts of: 'Yes!' and, 'Take her mask off! Take her mask off!'

'My lords, ladies and gentlemen!' boomed the MC, flinging his arm towards the curtains at the back of the hall. 'Let's have a huge Riverdam Slam welcome for . . . the Masked

Avenger!'

The curtains parted and into the hall stepped Princess Ava dressed as the Masked Avenger. Her costume was purple and she wore a hood with two eyeholes in it completely covering her head. The crowd continued chanting 'Take her mask off! Take her mask off!' as Princess Ava ran down the aisle, somersaulted over the ropes into the ring to land nimbly on her feet, and then did another somersault into the centre of the ring.

She saluted the crowd as the MC announced: 'The rules: the first to get two pinfalls or two submissions, or a knockout, is the winner! And now – let the action begin!'

The bell by the side of the ring sounded.

The Riverdam Slam had begun!

CHAPTER 3

The Masked Avenger darted out of her corner and threw herself at Grit. Jack winced and half-closed his eyes in anticipation of the Avenger crashing into the small, solid rocky figure, but instead the Avenger surprised everyone, including Grit, by suddenly dropping to the floor seconds before she hit Grit and sliding into the small troll's shins, grabbing them with both hands. She then slid around behind Grit, pulling back to try and pull the troll over.

It didn't work. Grit used her weight and her low centre of gravity to remain solidly upright. Then she reached down, grabbed the Avenger by one arm and threw her up into the air, caught her as she came down, and hurled her hard at the nearest corner post.

The Masked Avenger thudded into the post and crashed to the canvas.

'Ouch!' winced Jack. 'That must have hurt.'

The Avenger went into the attack again, this time jumping high and leaping onto Grit's shoulders, her feet gripping Grit's head on either side. Then the Avenger tried a forward roll, but again Grit used her weight and low centre of gravity to stand still, like a rock. Grit slammed her hands up to clap the Avenger's ankles to the sides of her head, and the Avenger found herself upside down with her feet trapped in Grit's rocky fists.

BANG!

Grit slammed the Masked Avenger head first down onto the canvas twice, and then let go of her ankles.

The Avenger, dazed by the double blow to the top of her head, fell down onto the canvas, and immediately Grit fell on her, pinning both the Avenger's shoulders to the canvas.

'One!' shouted the crowd approvingly, as the Master of Ceremonies (now the referee) began the count. 'Two! Three!'

Grit pushed herself up off the fallen Avenger and returned to her corner, while the crowd erupted with shouts of 'Grit! Grit! Grit' and 'Take her mask off!'

'It's not looking good,' said Jack, worried.

The Masked Avenger pushed herself off the canvas. To Jack, she still looked groggy, wobbling slightly as she stood up. The crowd sensed it and began shouting for Grit to finish the job.

'Go for her!' they yelled excitedly.

Jack, concerned, watched the Avenger stumble unsteadily. Grit saw this, and moved, throwing herself directly at the Avenger, intending to knock her to the canvas while she was still dazed and then fall on her, pinning her down once more to finish the bout.

It was then that Jack realised that the Avenger's wobbling was an act. Quick as a flash, the Avenger swayed sidways and Grit stumbled past her, unable to change direction. Her troll-weight, which had been a major advantage when holding the Avenger down to the canvas, now put her at a disadvantage. The Avenger leapt into the air and thudded the soles of both her feet hard against Grit's back, sending her plummeting forward into the ropes and being bounced back. As Grit stumbled backwards, trying to regain her balance, the Masked Avenger slid past her, catching her behind the

knees, and the troll fell.

Immediately, the Avenger dropped on Grit's head, smothering her and holding her head and neck down firmly on the canvas, the troll's own weight pinioning her shoulders down.

'One! Two! Three!' called the referee, and the crowd erupted into applause again as this time the Masked Avenger got to her feet and strode away from her fallen opponent.

One pinfall each!

The rest of the contest was a battle that swung first in Grit's favour, then in the Masked Avenger's, as the two wrestlers threw themselves at one another, and tried every hold and throw in their repertoire to get the final winning throw on their opponent.

The end, when it came, was nimbleness over strength. Grit had gripped the Avenger in a bear hug, squeezing her between her powerful arms, trying for a submission. The Avenger heaved herself backwards and managed to put Grit off-balance; but the troll held on grimly as the two toppled to the canvas, with the

Avenger in a vulnerable position beneath the troll and looking as if she was about to be pinned for the final fall. But suddenly, the Avenger pushed up with her feet against Grit's body, and then let the troll crash back down hard to the canvas, the troll's weight making the canvas bounce, sending the Avenger springing up enough to be able to spin nimbly out of the troll's grip.

Before Grit knew what was happening, the Avenger had spun the troll over onto her back, and then pulled Grit's legs up as far as she could towards Grit's face, the weight of Grit's legs helping to keep her held down.

'One!' roared the crowd.

'Two!' called the referee. And then: 'Three!' And it was over.

The two wrestlers clambered to their feet, and shook hands, as the Referee announced: 'And the winner, with two pinfalls, is the Masked Avenger!'

CHAPTER 4

'Looks like Ava gets to keep her mask on,' Jack whispered to Milo as they headed to the dressing room, where Big Rock and Sam were waiting.

The interval had been declared, and the crowd had flooded out of the hall to get a breath of fresh air, or grab a snack, before the main bout: the tag event between Big Rock and Sam, and the two orcs.

As Jack and Milo were about to walk into the dressing room, they were barged aside by two large orcs. They both wore identical red and black costumes.

'So!' sneered one, looking at Big Rock and Sam. 'You must be our opponents! Or, as we call them, losers!'

At this, both orcs threw their heads back and laughed gloating, cackling laughs. Then they turned to one another and clashed their claws together, sparks flying from them.

'See you in the ring, losers!' growled the other orc.

With that, they left the room.

'I guess those are our opponents,' said Sam. 'Slash and Burn.'

'Orcs!' snorted Big Rock derisively, and he made a fart noise again.

After the usual introductions in the ring by the Master of Ceremonies, with different sections of the crowd showing their support for the separate tag teams, the waving of placards, the chanting and singing of their favourites' names, the bout got underway. The rules of tag wrestling were simple: one wrestler from each team in the ring at one time; with their partner outside on the apron of the ring, leaning on the ropes. To change wrestlers, the one in the ring had to touch – or 'tag' – the hand of his partner outside the ring; at which point they changed over: the one in the ring coming out, and the other coming into the ring, to carry on the battle.

From the outset, the two orcs started breaking the rules, with both of them in the ring at the same time, attacking Big Rock when he was in on his own. The referee immediately ordered one of the orcs out of the ring, at which the orcs' supporters began protesting and booing loudly. At first it looked as if neither orc would leave, but then Sam reached into the ring, grabbed Slash and hauled him over the ropes and dumped him out of the ring, on the floor of the hall near the front row of seats.

In the ring, Big Rock grabbed hold of Burn, turned him upside down and slammed him head first into the canvas. The orc was tough, though. Instead of collapsing, Burn kicked out with both feet and sent the big troll staggering backwards towards the ropes. Slash had returned and immediately leant forward, grabbed hold of Big Rock and pulled him back, then wrapped the top rope around the troll's neck.

Burn bounced forward in a high leap and kicked the trapped Big Rock hard in the chest with both feet, while Slash raked his sharp talons across Big Rock's skull. Both orcs then started to thump Big Rock, while the troll struggled to extricate himself from the rope.

Sam had been calling angrily for the referee to intervene, but despite the referee trying to call the two orcs to order, Slash and Burn carried on pounding Big Rock. Furious, Sam also decided to ignore the rules. He leapt into the ring, marched up to Burn, grabbed hold of the orc and threw him out of the ring to land among a group of orc supporters crowded in an aisle.

Sam helped Big Rock untangle himself from

the ropes, then both went back to their corner and waited for the two orcs to scramble back into theirs. The orcs were furious, both complaining loudly to the referee about Sam, waving their claws angrily and demanding that Sam and Big Rock be disqualified, but the referee shook his head and pointed them to return to their corner.

This time it was Slash and Sam who took to the ring, with Big Rock and Burn pacing around the apron, watching and waiting to be tagged and called into action.

Slash did his best to live up to his name, slashing at Sam with his sharp talons, but Sam kept ducking and dodging, and the orc's claws whistled by him, just missing by a whisker each time. All the while, Sam kept moving, in a crouch, waiting for the right moment to grab the orc, but very aware of those sharp claws.

On the ropes, Burn growled, frustrated by the failure of his partner to land a cutting blow on Sam. Suddenly Burn gave an eerie sound, a sharp whistle. It was obviously a signal for some kind of concerted action, because Slash stopped waving his claws and trying to mark Sam. Instead, he smiled, and then suddenly launched himself head first at Sam, his head aimed like a cannon ball. Jack had already seen how hard the top of an orc's skull was from earlier in the bout, when Big Rock had slammed Burn head first into the canvas, with no effect.

At the same time, Burn hurled himself into the ring head first, also aiming at Sam, and Jack realised with horror that the orcs were intending to crush Sam between their hard skulls, like two hammers crashing together.

'Behind you!' shouted Big Rock in warning, but Sam had obviously been expecting something like this because he dropped like a stone, and the two orcs collided hard skull against hard skull above him.

The collision of the two orcs smashing their heads against one another was felt all the way round the hall. Some people shuddered at the sound of the impact, others gasped in shock.

The two orcs crashed to the canvas and lay

there, head to head, their arms and legs twitching slightly, but otherwise they were out cold.

The referee began his count: 'One. Two. Three . . .' By the time he reached seven, the two orcs had just begun to move slightly, but

they were too dazed to do much more than try to push themselves up, and they slumped down to the canvas again as the referee finished his count: 'Eight. Nine. Ten! And I declare the winners of this tag event to be: Big Rock and Sam Dent!'

CHAPTER 5

Milo and Jack joined Big Rock and Sam in the dressing room.

'Fantastic!' Milo congratulated them. 'Fair play won! The cheats lost!'

'They certainly did!' said a voice.

They turned and saw that Hunk had arrived and was smiling broadly at Big Rock and Sam. 'You two work so well together. You should stay as a tag team! You'd be awesome!'

'Unfortunately, I can't do that,' said Sam ruefully. 'I love wrestling, but I've got a full-time job, helping Princess Ava run the Kingdom of Weevil. We're just getting it back on its feet after a revolution there.'

'He *Sir* Sam Dent,' said Big Rock. 'Big

important man.'

'Wow!' said Hunk, impressed.

'Like I say, I wrestle when I can, but helping Princess Ava is hard work.'

'She's tough, is she?' asked Hunk.

Sam grinned and winked at Jack and Milo.

'You've no idea how tough she is!' he smiled.

Hunk turned to Big Rock.

'Hey, then how about you and me?' he suggested.

'You and me what?' asked Big Rock, puzzled.

'As a tag team,' said Hunk. 'Tag-Wrestling Trolls! I am such a huge fan of yours, Big Rock! You are such an awesome wrestler! I hope one day to be as good as you, but in the meantime, I could learn from you as we work together! I'm already good, but I could be so much better! What do you say?'

Big Rock stared at Hunk in bewilderment, then at Jack and Milo. The big troll wasn't used to getting this sort of enthusiastic fan treatment.

'Well . . .' he began, still taken aback.

'It would be brilliant!' continued Hunk

enthusiastically. 'Awesome!' He turned to Milo and asked: 'What do you say, Milo?'

Milo hesitated and looked at Jack. 'What do you think, Jack?' he asked.

'It's a good *idea*,' Jack said carefully. Then he turned to Hunk and said: 'The only thing is, we haven't seen you wrestle yet, so we don't know what you're like.'

'You mean, if I'm any good,' said Hunk.

'No,' said Jack quickly, and he wondered if it was obvious that he was lying. 'I mean, we don't know what your style is, and how it would work with Big Rock.'

Hunk grinned. 'Trust me, I am a fantastic wrestler! Strong, tough, courageous, with some great moves! And I am a troll! And the sign on your caravan says WWT – Waldo's Wrestling Trolls! At the moment you've only got one.'

'Good point,' nodded Big Rock. 'Need more trolls.'

'It'll be perfect!' beamed Hunk.

'Er . . .' said Milo awkwardly. 'Yes, it's a good

idea . . .'

'Great!' boomed Big Rock happily.

'. . . but I need to think about it.'

Big Rock frowned.

'What to think about?'

'Er . . . the billing. Contracts. That sort of thing,' said Milo lamely.

'I understand!' smiled Hunk. 'Business! You think about it, Milo, and let us know. Me and Big Rock can't wait to get in that ring as a tag team!' He clapped Big Rock on the shoulder. 'Come on, Big Rock. Let's go and get some granite pebbles to munch, while Milo thinks about it.'

Milo and Jack watched as Big Rock and Hunk walked away to the refreshment tent.

'Well?' asked Milo, when the two wrestlers were out of earshot.

'In theory it's a good idea,' said Jack. 'Troll tag wrestlers. Like Hunk said, it's what it says on the caravan.'

'But . . . ?' queried Milo.

'Hunk could be a fake,' said Robin, appearing

beside them. 'He talks about being a great wrestler, but we've never seen him in action. He could be planning to use Big Rock to get his career going: Big Rock does the wrestling in the ring, and all Hunk does is pose.'

Milo and Jack nodded thoughtfully at this.

'The trouble is, Big Rock's all excited about the idea. He won't be happy if we say no to him and Hunk as a tag team,' continued Jack unhappily. 'So, how do we say no without upsetting Big Rock?'

Milo sighed gloomily.

'I'm his manager, I guess that's up to me to handle,' he said.

CHAPTER 6

Milo and Jack found Big Rock on the green outside the Town Hall. Big Rock was signing autographs for fans, pressing his thumbprint into their autograph books. Hunk was telling the waiting fans that he and Big Rock were going to be appearing as a troll tag team.

Milo and Jack detached Big Rock from the fans and took him and Hunk to their caravan.

'We think you two as a tag team is a great idea!' said Milo. 'Fantastic!'

'Great!' beamed Big Rock.

'Brilliant!' grinned Hunk.

'But first, we think it would be a good idea to see you in the ring together. You know, a friendly bout, just to see Hunk in action.'

'Excellent!' smiled Hunk. 'When?'

'How about today?' said Milo. 'After all, the ring's still in place.'

'Awesome!' said Hunk. 'How about we do it in an hour, to give me time to get limbered up. I like to do a practice run to get myself fit.'

'Fine,' said Milo.

'I come with you!' suggested Big Rock enthusiastically. 'We do practice run together.'

Hunk gave Big Rock an apologetic smile.

'I'm sorry, Big Rock,' he said. 'The thing is, I also meditate while I run. So, please don't take offence, but I like to do my meditation run on my own.'

Big Rock frowned.

'Meditate?' he repeated, puzzled.

'I get in touch with my inner troll,' said Hunk. 'Is that okay with you?'

'Sure,' nodded Big Rock.

'Cool,' said Hunk. 'I'll see you at the ring in an hour.'

With that, Hunk set off, his big troll feet pounding away on the grass. Big Rock watched him go.

'He meditate,' he told Milo and Jack.

'So we heard,' said Milo.

Big Rock frowned.

'What means meditate?' he asked.

'It means . . . er . . . thinking,' said Milo. 'Deep thinking.'

'Ah,' nodded Big Rock.

He stood there, silent, for a few seconds, then announced: 'I done thinking. Now I go and practise and get ready.'

And with that, the huge troll started going through some moves to limber up, while Milo and Jack watched.

'What do you think?' whispered Milo to Jack.

'I think we wait and see how Hunk does in the ring,' said Jack.

'Meditation run!' scoffed a voice beside them.

They turned and saw that Robin had joined them.

'You heard all that?' asked Milo.

'Of course,' said Robin. 'The man's a poser!'

'Hey!' called a voice.

They turned and saw Sam Dent and Princess Ava heading towards them.

'What's this I hear about a match between Big Rock and Hunk?' asked Ava. 'Hunk just told us about it. Is he making it up?'

'It's true,' said Jack. 'They're going into the ring together as soon as Hunk gets back from his practice run.'

'This I have to see!' said Ava eagerly. 'We were about to head back to Weevil, but when we heard about this . . .'

'Not to be missed!' nodded Sam in agreement.

'At least we'll find out whether Hunk is a real wrestler or a fake,' Milo muttered to Jack.

Inside the Town Hall, Jack and the gang watched as Big Rock did press-ups and generally limbered up. A few of the townspeople had wandered in, curious to see this unofficial extra bout. As word spread, Jack noticed even more people arriving and grabbing a seat.

The only person not there was Hunk.

Milo looked at his watch.

'Hunk should be here by now,' he said.

Robin snorted. 'He's chickened out,' he said. 'Like I said, he's just a poser. I bet he's never wrestled.'

The sound of the door opening made them all look round, and they saw Hunk appear. He had an apologetic smile on his face. His left arm was in a sling.

'Hi, guys!' he said as he walked down the aisle and joined them. He gestured at the sling on his arm. 'It looks like the match is off, I'm afraid. I injured my arm.'

'While meditating?' asked Robin, a sarcastic note in his voice.

'Stopping a runaway horse,' said Hunk. 'It

had a small child on its back and it was out of control, so I jumped in its path and pulled it to a halt.' He gave a sigh. 'Unfortunately, I wrenched my arm doing it.'

'That was a very brave thing to do,' said Jack. Hunk shrugged.

'It was nothing,' he said. 'It's just unfortunate that I can't go into the ring with Big Rock until my injured arm gets better.'

'Not to worry,' said Big Rock. 'Accidents happen. You join us anyway. We still be tag team.'

'Er . . .' said Milo cautiously. 'It's not that easy, Big Rock.'

'Why?' demanded Big Rock.

'We need to see Hunk actually *wrestle*,' said Milo.

'But he can't,' said Big Rock. 'He hurt arm saving small child from runaway horse!'

'Yes, well . . .' began Milo awkwardly.

'You don't believe me,' sighed Hunk.

'I never said that!' defended Milo.

'You didn't need to,' said Hunk. He gave a

rueful smile. 'Don't worry,' he said. 'I absolutely understand your position, Milo. I'd be suspicious as well, if I was you, in these circumstances.'

Big Rock frowned as he looked at Milo and Jack.

'You think Hunk telling lie?' he asked, annoyed.

'Well . . .' began Milo, embarrassed.

'I think they think I might have made it up about being a wrestler,' said Hunk. 'Or exaggerated how good I am.' He gave a laugh. 'And you can see their point of view. When I'm

forced to prove it, I injure my arm!' He smiled at Milo and Jack. 'As I say, I'm not upset. I only wish I had the chance to prove you wrong. But . . .'

'You say Hunk lie!' said Big Rock, and now they could see the big troll was really upset.

'We never said that, Big Rock,' appealed Jack. 'But, as Hunk says himself, we've never actually seen him wrestle . . .'

'He say he's good,' growled big Rock. 'That good enough for me!'

'Yes, but, just because someone says they're good, it doesn't mean they are,' said Milo. 'I mean, I could *say* I'm a brilliant wrestler, but it doesn't mean I am.'

'You not brilliant wrestler,' said Big Rock, looking puzzled at this turn of the conversation.

'Exactly, that's the point I'm trying to make,' said Milo.

Big Rock scowled.

'Trolls don't lie,' he said. 'And Hunk is troll!'

'Half-troll,' put in Robin. 'Like Jack.'

Hunk looked at Jack, intrigued.

'You're a half-troll like me?' he said, impressed. 'Which part?'

'All of him,' said Milo.

'But I'm not the same as you,' said Jack. 'When I turn into a troll, all of me turns troll. From the top of my head to the bottom of my feet.'

'He turns into Thud,' added Big Rock. 'Big strong troll. Stronger than me.'

'Wow!' said Hunk, awed. 'I'd like to see that!'

'We all would,' said Milo, 'but it doesn't happen a lot.'

'And I can't make it happen,' said Jack. 'It just sort of . . . happens. Now and then.'

'When things are bad,' said Big Rock. 'When we're in trouble. And there's big danger.'

'Awesome!' said Hunk. He gave a big smile. 'We could be a triple troll tag team: Big Rock, Hunk and Thud!'

'No!' snapped Big Rock, still upset. 'They call you liar!' He shook his head. 'Me and Hunk make troll tag team on our own.'

Milo and Jack gaped at their big troll friend.

'But Big Rock . . . !' Milo began to protest.

Big Rock shook his head.

'Me and Hunk be troll tag team on our own,' Big Rock repeated. 'Come on, Hunk.'

With that, Big Rock turned and stomped away.

Hunk looked awkward and embarrassed.

'Actually, I don't think you should be too hasty, Big Rock!' he called after the big troll, but Big Rock kept walking, a cloud of upsetness hanging over him. Hunk turned back to Milo, Jack and Robin and gave an apologetic smile. 'I'm sorry about that,' he said. 'I think he got upset because we're both trolls. It's a brotherhood thing. I'll have a word with him and sort it out.'

And with that, Hunk hurried after Big Rock.

'Huh! Well, you messed that up!' snorted Robin.

'What else could I say?' asked Milo defensively.

'You know how sensitive Big Rock is,' said Princess Ava accusingly, coming forward for the first time.

'Yes, but Milo was on a loser,' put in Sam, defending Milo. 'Whatever Milo said, he would have been in the wrong, unless he said yes to Hunk joining the group.'

'Don't worry, Big Rock will come back,' said Milo confidently. 'We've been together too long for him to walk out just like that.'

'And Hunk said he was going to talk to him,' Jack reminded them.

'Yes, but it depends on what Hunk actually says to Big Rock,' said Robin thoughtfully. 'All that being friendly and apologising and flattering, maybe it was all part of an act to get Big Rock away from Milo.'

'Well, it looks like he succeeded,' snorted Princess Ava. She turned to Sam. 'It looks like there's not going to be anything else interesting happening, so we might as well head back to Weevil.'

'Yes, Your Highness,' nodded Sam.

'Sam, please,' sighed Ava. 'You only need to call me Your Highness when we're at an official function.'

'What does he call you when you're not?' asked Jack.

'The Masked Avenger, of course!' said Ava. 'Come on, Sam. The royal coach is waiting for us!'

CHAPTER 7

As Jack, Milo and Robin walked away from their caravan, Milo let out a long and unhappy sigh.

'So, I guess that's it!' he said miserably. 'If Big Rock leaves to join Hunk, that'll be the end of Waldo's Wrestling Trolls. Big Rock was the very last of the Wrestling Trolls.'

'He'll be back,' said Jack. 'You said so yourself.'

'I was just saying that to cheer myself up,' admitted Milo. 'You saw the expression on his face, and what he said. He wants to leave and join Hunk. That's it. Waldo's Wrestling Trolls is over. Finished.'

'There's always Thud,' suggested Robin.

'No,' said Milo, shaking his head. 'We never know when Jack's going to turn into him. How can we advertise Thud the Wrestling Troll when ninety-nine per cent of the time he's just Jack.'

'Maybe I can learn how to control it?' said Jack hopefully.

'How?' asked Milo.

Jack gave an unhappy shrug.

'I don't know,' he admitted miserably.

Suddenly they heard the fast pounding of hooves behind them, and a voice shouting, 'Help! Help! The dam!'

They turned, and saw a panic-stricken looking man on a galloping horse arrive on the green. The man leapt off the horse and ran to Milo, Jack and Robin.

'We need help!' he exclaimed. 'The dam's breaking! If it gives way, the valley and all the towns in it will be flooded!' shouted the man urgently. 'Everyone will be killed!'

The man's frantic yells had brought Princess Ava and Sam Dent hurrying back, and Jack could see that Big Rock and Hunk were also running towards them, anxious expressions on their faces.

'We need to put logs in the breach and tie them in place!' said the frightened man.

'We do that!' said Big Rock. 'Come! Quick!'

'I'm with you, Big Rock!' nodded Sam Dent, and then he, along with Princess Ava and Hunk with his arm still in a sling, ran after the big troll towards the dam. Jack noticed that, as Princess Ava ran, she was taking her mask from a pocket and pulling it over her head.

'Let's see what we can do to help!' urged Milo.

As Milo, Jack and Robin followed the others, Milo said to Jack: 'Maybe you'll turn into Thud. It sounds like we're going to need Thud's strength.'

'It doesn't feel like it's going to happen,' said Jack unhappily.

When he was about to turn into Thud, Jack usually felt a tingly sensation run through his body, and his vision became filmy as a thin layer of transparent rock covered his eyes. Right now there was no tingly sensation – he was still just small, nine-year-old Jack.

As they got near to the dam, Jack realised for the first time how big it was. It was indeed very much like the crude sort of dam that beavers built, but massive. It was made from whole trees piled into the river, and then more trees and huge logs laid on them, each one tied in place by thick ropes. Some of the trees had been kept alive by the water seeping through the cracks in the dam, and smaller trees and bushes had sprouted out from the original logs and trees, so that the whole dam looked like a high mountain wall of living greenery.

Now, in the middle of this massive mountain of logs and trees and bushes, a gap had opened up and water was gushing through. The ropes holding the trees together in the centre must have rotted, or become dislodged. Whatever the reason, the force of the water pouring through the gap had started to make the rest of the trees and logs around the gap unsafe. Even as Jack watched, a whole tree came away from the middle of the wall and tumbled down, rolling over and over before it crashed into the river below. The additional force of water had turned the previously peaceful river into a raging torrent. Jack could only guess at the incredibly powerful force of water behind the huge wooden dam, pressing against it, punching holes in it. More gaps were opening up in the giant wall of wood as logs suddenly hurtled out from the dam like bullets shot from a gun, and more water gushed through the new gap and poured down the dam.

The river below the dam was rising rapidly and was almost up to the level of the riverbanks. Very soon it would be pouring over the banks and begin cascading towards the town, and then on through the rest of the valley to the other towns and villages, drowning them, and the people and animals who lived there.

Already, many of the townsfolk were climbing over the huge dam, clinging onto the slippery logs and trees and trying to tie the loose wood into place. The dam was so big the people looked like insects as they clambered up the wall of timber, ropes wrapped around them so they could tie the trees to one another and try to stabilise the dam.

Big Rock, Sam Dent, Princess Ava (as the Masked Avenger) and Grit were climbing up the dam to join those already on it, slipping now and then on the wet logs and trees, but steadfastly making their way towards the breach in the dam.

'Where's Hunk?' asked Jack. 'I can't see him. I thought he was with them.'

'Huh!' snorted Robin derisively. 'I bet he's hiding somewhere. And after it's all over he'll come out and tell stories about how brave he was. He's a fake wrestler and a fake hero.'

As they watched, another log spilled out from the hole in the dam and hurtled down to the river, hitting Grit. The young troll nearly fell, but the Masked Avenger stretched out an arm and grabbed her, pulling her to safety.

'They need more help!' said Jack.

'They need Thud,' said Milo. He looked at

Jack hopefully. 'Anything yet?'

Jack shook his head.

'No,' he said. 'It'll just have to be little me.'

'It'll be both of us,' said Milo.

'And me!' declared Robin.

Milo shook his head.

'Those logs and trees are soaking wet and slippery, you won't be able to get a grip on them with your hooves.'

'In that case, I'll help the townsfolk,' said Robin. He looked towards the town, where people were carrying their belongings out of their houses and loading them onto carts. 'They'll need a horse to pull the carts to higher ground if the dam breaks.'

With that, he galloped back towards the town.

There was a crashing sound behind them and Jack and Milo turned and saw another log had become detached from the middle of the dam and had tumbled into the river.

Quickly, Jack grabbed up a loop of thick rope from the pile lying by the riverbank and ran towards the bottom of the dam to join the others.

Jack and Milo climbed up the dam. It was hard work; the logs and trees beneath their feet were slippery, and the whole lot kept moving as the weight of water behind the dam tried to push through. Finally, they reached the widening crack in the middle of the dam.

Big Rock, Sam Dent, the Masked Avenger and Grit were working together as a team, passing the ends of ropes to one another along a chain they had formed, and wrapping and tying them around the trees. Jack and Milo worked their way along the mass of slippery logs and joined them.

But how much longer will those ropes hold? wondered Jack. And why can't I turn into Thud? If ever there was a dangerous life-threatening situation, then it's right here and now!

Grit passed a length of rope along to Jack, and as Jack reached out to take it and pass it along, there was a sudden *woosh!* and the section of dam right in front of Jack suddenly cracked open and a gush of water burst through, hitting Jack and sending him tumbling backwards, and away from the dam towards the river below.

For a second, Jack seemed to hang suspended, frantically stretching back at the dam and the ropes, and the others. But his hands just touched thin air.

And then he was falling!

CHAPTER 8

I'm going to die! Jack thought as he fell, and saw the river far below rushing up towards him . . .

SMACK!!!!

Something grabbed him around the chest, and then he was sailing upwards instead of falling downwards.

I'm flying, he realised.

He looked down, and realised that a massive pair of rock-like legs had wrapped themselves around him, with two enormous rock-like feet holding him securely. He looked up, and was astonished to see the friendly face of Hunk smiling down at him. The half-troll still had one arm in a sling, but with his good hand and

arm he was holding tightly onto a rope.

Hunk swung back towards the dam, and took the impact of the crash against the dam with his feet and legs, protecting Jack from the collision.

'Thanks, Hunk!' burst out Jack. 'You saved my life!'

'You'd have done the same for me," Hunk called up.

'Of course!' yelled Milo in realisation. The large net would hold the logs back far more securely than tying them together.

Milo, Jack and the Masked Avenger moved as swiftly as they could down the wall of timber. To speed things up, some of the townspeople had realised what was needed and grabbed the ends of the net and began to haul it up to where Milo, Jack and Ava could get hold of it.

They grabbed the net, and were just about to haul it up, when there was another sudden gush of water bursting through a new crack in the dam, this one just below them.

For the first time, Jack saw that a small boy had been in the group of townspeople that had scrambled up the wall of shaking timber, obviously doing his best to help the grown-ups haul the heavy net up the dam. The water struck the boy full in the chest, the same as Jack had been hit just a few moments before, and hurled him outwards.

Instinctively, Jack leapt out towards the boy, his hands grasping to try and save the boy, catch him, but Jack's grip on the dam wall vanished and Jack found himself falling . . . falling . . .

Jack couldn't even see the boy properly; the rush of water pouring past him filled his eyes. No, there was something more than that, a film was forming over his eyes, a glassy, brownish film. As he fell he felt a tingly sensation going through him, then he felt his hands grab something soft. It was the boy!

Still falling, Jack felt himself crash into the raging water and sink, going down, down, down, the boy still held in one hand . . .

And then Jack was suddenly standing up, his head clear of the water, his feet on the bottom of

the river. He realised that he was no longer short and thin Jack, submerged beneath the waters, but he was a very tall, very powerful troll.

He was Thud.

Thud stood in the raging river torrent as the waters poured around him, just beneath his chin. Above him, held aloft in one of his huge hands, was the small boy, soaking wet – but very much alive.

CHAPTER 9

Jack sat with Milo on the steps of the caravan, with Robin next to them.

It was all over. For the moment, at least, the danger had passed. The small boy was safe and well and had been taken home. The huge net had been fixed into place, holding the dam steady. The gushes of water had been reduced to a trickle.

With the dam made safe, Princess Ava and Sam Dent had left for Weevil, and now there was just Milo and Jack and Robin, watching as Big Rock and Hunk – still with one arm in a sling – hammered home the last of the huge steel pegs to fix key logs in place.

'So Hunk really did injure his arm stopping

a runaway horse,' sighed Milo gloomily.

'Yes,' nodded Robin. 'I met the horse that did it. He was very ashamed. He'd got a thistle stuck under his saddle, that's what made him bolt.'

'And Ug really did have stomach ache from something he'd eaten,' said Jack with an equally heavy sigh. 'Mushrooms. So it was nothing to do with Hunk.'

Robin snorted. 'Some people cause a lot of trouble by spreading wild and untrue stories,' he announced.

'And some horses as well,' said Milo pointedly.

Robin shook his head. 'I was just passing on information in good faith,' he said.

Milo and Jack again looked towards where Big Rock and Hunk had put down their tools.

'Big Rock won't forgive us for what we said about Hunk,' said Milo gloomily. 'And nor will Hunk.'

'You didn't actually *accuse* Hunk of lying,' said Jack.

'No, but we thought it,' said Milo, 'and that's

just as bad.' He let out a mournful sigh. 'I guess Big Rock and Hunk will now go off on their own and become the troll tag team.' He let out another sigh, even heavier than the last. 'It's the end of Waldo's Wrestling Trolls.'

'Not necessarily,' said Jack. 'Maybe Hunk will join us.'

'After the way we treated him?' said Milo scornfully.

'It's worth asking,' insisted Jack.

Milo sighed again.

'I suppose so,' he said.

They looked up as Big Rock and Hunk joined them.

'Dam mended!' announced Big Rock.

'Almost,' added Hunk. 'There's still a lot of work to be done to rebuild it.'

'But it safe for now,' said Big Rock.

Hunk looked at Jack and grinned.

'I see what Big Rock meant about Thud being so great!' he said. 'The way you dived down from the dam, and saved that little boy's life. Awesome!'

'Thud big hero,' nodded Big Rock approvingly.

Jack shook his head. 'No,' he said. 'You guys are the heroes. You were fantastic up there, working on that dam, saving the lives of the whole town.'

'Three hero trolls!' grinned Milo. 'Big Rock, Thud and Hunk!'

'What a great tag team that would make!' said Jack, grabbing the opportunity to bring the subject into the conversation. 'The Troll Tag Trio!'

'A great idea,' said Hunk. Then he gave a sigh. 'But I don't think it's on.'

'No,' admitted Milo. 'I can see your point of view, Hunk, and why you wouldn't want to join us. We were horrible to you. We doubted you and . . .'

'Oh no!' said Hunk quickly. 'Nothing like that! I don't blame you at all! The fact is I'd love to join you and WWT. But, as I was just saying to Big Rock, I've decided to stay here and help the townspeople rebuild their dam. They need me. It's going to take some time, but once it's over . . .'

'Hunk says he join us later,' nodded Big Rock happily. 'Me and him be tag team together. Milo be our manager. We be part of Waldo's Wrestling Trolls.'

Milo beamed with a smile so wide that Jack thought it was going to split his face in half.

'That's fantastic!' he said. 'Brilliant!'

'Anyway, me and Big Rock are going to get something to eat,' said Hunk. 'All that hard work has made me hungry.'

'Good idea!' said Big Rock. 'They got nice granite in kitchen!'

As the troll and the half-troll strode off towards the kitchen in the Town Hall, Milo gave a huge sigh of relief.

'Hurrah! We're still Waldo's Wrestling Trolls!' he said, delightedly.

Robin nodded sagely.

'I always knew that Hunk was a good guy really,' he said.

Don't miss these other exciting adventures from Hot Key Books ...

THE GREAT GALLOON

TOM BANKS

The Great Galloon is an enormous airship, built by Captain Meredith Anstruther and manned by his crew, who might seem like a bit of a motley bunch but who are able to fight off invading marauders whilst drinking tea and sweeping floors!

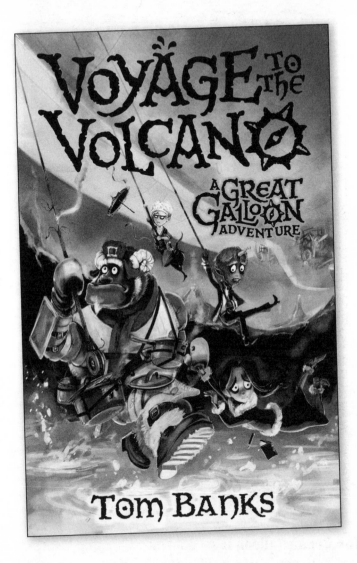

Captain Anstruther and his motley crew of
sky-pirates are back for more adventures!

A squirrel, a hot dog stand, the planet Jupiter...
what will get shrunk next?

THE SUNDAY TIMES 'Book of the Week'

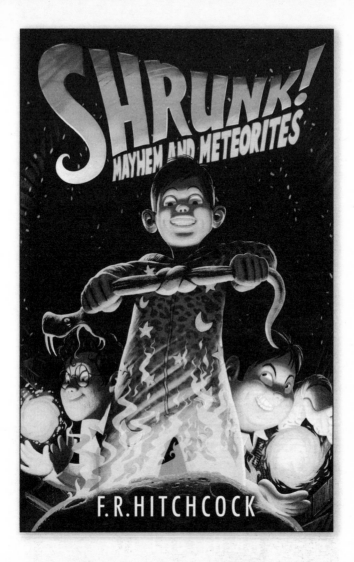

SHRUNK!
MAYHEM AND METEORITES

F.R.HITCHCOCK

All is quiet in the sleepy seaside town of Bywater-by-Sea
- that is, until two meteorites fall to earth -
landing in the middle of the Field Craft Troop's
outdoor expedition camp.

Uniquely written by 2000 children and Fleur Hitchcock
in the online live writing project, TheStoryAdventure.com

Lovereading4kids reader reviews of
Wrestling Trolls Match 1: Big Rock and the Masked Avenger
by Jim Eldridge

'I really like Wrestling Trolls. I really like Robin the horse because he talks, Big Rock because he's nice, Jack because he saves Princess Ava, and Princess Ava because she wrestles!'
Richie, age 7

'Wrestling Trolls is an action-packed book with awesome wrestling moves. The characters are clever and funny. I loved the story and can't wait to read the next instalment.'
Jacob, age 9

'The story had funny parts, action and good characters. Some of my favourite parts were Jack turning into a wrestling troll and I liked Robin the horse because he was grumpy and helpful.'
Jack, age 8

'It was brilliant! I liked how Jack changed into Thud – I won't tell you what Thud is so I don't give away the story . . . I really liked the song and keep singing it.'
George, age 7

'Wrestling Trolls is exciting because it is full of action. This book is fantastic if you like lots of wrestling and people being rescued from bad guys.'
Thomas, age 7

'I give it 10/10 even though I don't like wrestling, because I liked the story!'
Alexander, age 8